O9-AIE-978

For both Charlottes

**Produced by the Department of Publications
The Museum of Modern Art, New York**

**Christopher Hudson, Publisher
Chul R. Kim, Associate Publisher
David Frankel, Editorial Director
Marc Sapir, Production Director**

**11 West 53 Street
New York, NY 10019-5497
www.moma.org**

**Special thanks to Anne Morra, Associate
Curator in MoMA's Department of Film, for
her invaluable contribution to this book.**

**This book is dedicated to the memory of
Jytte Jensen, Curator in the Department of Film
at MoMA from 1982 to 2015.**

Written, illustrated and designed by Frank Viva

**Edited by Chul R. Kim and Emily Hall with
the generous participation of Cari Frisch,
Hannah Kim, Elizabeth Margulies, Françoise Mouly,
Susan Rich, Rajendra Roy, Charlie Scott,
Amanda Washburn, and Wendy Woon**

Production by Frank Viva and Chul R. Kim

This book is typeset in MoMA Gothic and Franklin.
The paper is 150 gsm woodfree.

© 2015 Frank Viva
First edition 2015
Library of Congress Control Number 2015941163
ISBN: 978-0-87070-950-0

Distributed in the United States and Canada
by Abrams Books for Young Readers,
an imprint of ABRAMS, New York

Distributed outside the United States and Canada
by Thames & Hudson Ltd.

Printed in Korea by Taeshin Inpack Co. Ltd.

YOUNG Charlotte FILMMAKER

The Museum of Modern Art, New York

Charlotte is a filmmaker. She takes her camera everywhere she goes and shoots movies of everything she sees—as long as it's black and white.

Mostly, she likes to film her tomcat, Smudge. Never was there a cat so black. Some people—usually adults—mistake Smudge for nothing more than black ink on paper. That's crazy!

At school, when Charlotte tells Mister Puce that her favorite colors are black and white, he tells her that black and white are not colors at all—"they're opposites."

COOL!

Charlotte doesn't really care what they're called. She just wants to take a straw and drink all the color right out of the air.

Charlotte wishes that others could see just how wonderful black and white can be.

1, 2, 3...

But not on Friday nights, because that's when her mom and dad take her to see old black-and-white movies at the Golden Theatre, where, as her dad says, "The floors are sticky and the popcorn is icky."

Charlotte loves Sundays because she gets to go to The Museum of Modern Art with her mom and dad.

This Sunday, Charlotte is fascinated by a lady dressed in black and white who is looking at black-and-white art.

In no time at all, they become best friends.

I THINK MOVIES ARE MASTERPIECES.

Scarlet shows Charlotte all of her favorite films, including one called The Adventures of Prince Achmed. It was made a long time ago, when all films were black and white.

THIS WAS MADE WITH SHADOW PUPPETS. DO YOU LIKE IT?

Scarlet inspires Charlotte to make more and better movies. Black-and-white movies.

When Charlotte shows Scarlet
her latest film, Smudge, Scarlet
can't contain her excitement.

The next day, Charlotte arrives at the screening in a long black car that the Museum has sent. Waiting for her are hordes of colorful people. **HORDES!**

In the theater, Charlotte sits down beside Scarlet. When the movie begins, she doesn't like what all the colorful people are saying.

When the film ends and Charlotte lifts her head, there is only silence. It is the sort of serious silence that people call a dead silence. Then slowly (very slowly) a few people begin to clap. Then more. Then even more.

THEATRE

BOX
OFFICE →

STAGE

WOW

Famous

The next day, the whole colorful city is talking about Charlotte's film. Even the kids at her school show up and embrace Charlotte in all her black-and-whiteness. Charlotte embraces them, too.

Trustees of The Museum of Modern Art

David Rockefeller*
Honorary Chairman

Ronald S. Lauder
Honorary Chairman

Robert B. Menschel*
Chairman Emeritus

Agnes Gund*
President Emerita

Donald B. Marron
President Emeritus

Jerry I. Speyer
Chairman

Marie-Josée Kravis
President

Sid R. Bass
Vice Chairman

Leon D. Black
Vice Chairman

Mimi Haas
Vice Chairman

Richard E. Salomon
Vice Chairman

Glenn D. Lowry
Director

Richard E. Salomon
Treasurer

James Gara
Assistant Treasurer

Patty Lipshutz
Secretary

Wallis Annenberg

Lin Arison**

Sid R. Bass

Lawrence B. Benenson

Leon D. Black

Eli Broad*

Clarissa Alcock Bronfman

Patricia Phelps de Cisneros

Mrs. Jan Cowles**

Douglas S. Cramer*

Paula Crown

Lewis B. Cullman**

David Dechman

Glenn Dubin

Joel S. Ehrenkranz*

John Elkann

Laurence D. Fink

H.R.H. Duke Franz of Bavaria**

Glenn Fuhrman

Kathleen Fuld

Gianluigi Gabetti*

Howard Gardner

Maurice R. Greenberg**

Anne Dias Griffin

Agnes Gund*

Mimi Haas

Alexandra A. Herzan

Marlene Hess

Ronnie Heyman

AC Hudgins

Barbara Jakobson*

Werner H. Kramarsky*

Jill Kraus

Marie-Josée Kravis

June Noble Larkin*

Ronald S. Lauder

Thomas H. Lee

Michael Lynne

Donald B. Marron*

Wynton Marsalis**

Robert B. Menschel*

Philip S. Niarchos

James G. Niven

Peter Norton

Daniel S. Och

Maja Oeri

Richard E. Oldenburg**

Michael S. Ovitz

Ronald O. Perelman

Peter G. Peterson*

Emily Rauh Pulitzer*

David Rockefeller*

David Rockefeller, Jr.

Sharon Percy Rockefeller

Lord Rogers of Riverside**

Richard E. Salomon

Marcus Samuelsson

Ted Sann**

Anna Marie Shapiro*

Gilbert Silverman**

Anna Deavere Smith

Jerry I. Speyer

Ricardo Steinbruch

Yoshio Taniguchi**

Eugene V. Thaw**

Jeanne C. Thayer*

Alice M. Tisch

Joan Tisch*

Edgar Wachenheim III*

Gary Winnick

Ex Officio

Glenn D. Lowry
Director

Agnes Gund*
Chairman of the Board of MoMA PS1

Sharon Percy Rockefeller
President of The International Council

Christopher Lee Apgar and
Ann Schaffer
Co-Chairmen of The Contemporary Arts Council

Bill de Blasio
Mayor of the City of New York

Scott M. Stringer
Comptroller of the City of New York

Melissa Mark-Viverito
Speaker of the Council of the City of New York

*Life Trustee
**Honorary Trustee

Some of the people and things that Charlotte saw at The Museum of Modern Art

Department of Film

The Museum of Modern Art's Department of Film was founded in 1935, and since then it has collected nearly thirty thousand films of all types, from those made in the earliest days of cinema to those made in the present. The collection includes many curious and unusual works in black and white and color, such as Andy Warhol's eight-hour-long film of the Empire State Building at night; experimental works by Stan Brakhage, who drew and painted directly on filmstock; a Western by Clint Eastwood; and Tim Burton's *Edward Scissorhands*.

AT THE MUSEUM, WE THINK FILM IS ART.

Lotte Reiniger

Lotte Reiniger was a German filmmaker who pioneered the development of animated films in the 1920s. Her 1926 film, *The Adventures of Prince Achmed,* is the oldest surviving animated feature film. Reiniger invented a technique using cutout silhouettes. The film's story, based on elements taken from *The Thousand and One Nights*, relates the adventures of Prince Achmed as he battles an evil magician and falls in love with Peri Banu, the ruler of Wak Wak.

Jean (Hans) Arp

Jean (Hans) Arp was a French-German sculptor, painter, and writer. A pioneer of abstract art, he helped found the Dada movement and was involved in early Surrealist art. Arp also published essays and poetry. In many of his works he tried to create art influenced by nature and chance—free of human intervention.

Find out more about The Museum of Modern Art at MoMA.org.

BIG TOP

AVA...

MEAT

HOTEL
ENTRANCE →

PIZZA

DISCOUNT PRICES

ECON-O WASH

BOX OFFICE →

GOLDEN

THEATRE

ANASTASIA COURT

MARKET

BIJO

LOWER LEVEL

REAR W

Subway

SoHo